A Father's Guide to Loving your Neighbor as Yourself

Written by Stan Rawls

All credit of the project goes to our Lord and Savior Jesus Christ

Andrew "Kelly" Rawls

In Memory of our Dear Son

Andrew "Kelly" Rawls

April 22, 1987 to September 24, 2022

We love you!

Mom and Dad

Contents

Chapter 1 A Playoff Game to Remember

It was a crisp November day, the chill hinting at the arrival of winter. The sky was clear with a scattering of fluffy white clouds, and the golden sunlight lit up the colorful fallen leaves. It was the ideal day for football.

The South Charlotte Saints were facing the Riverside Raiders in a youth football league playoff game. The stands were packed as many anxious parents had come to see their sons play. On the sidelines, cheerleaders enthusiastically cheered for their teams. The stakes couldn't have been higher. The winner of this game would go on to play in the championship game in two weeks.

Both teams came in with impressive 9-1 records. The score was tied 14 to 14, and it was late in the 4th quarter. The clock showed only 1 minute and 25 seconds left in the game. The Saints had a 1st and 10 on the Raiders 30-yard line. Kelly Rawls, the Saints quarterback, broke the team from the huddle and led them to the line of scrimmage. They were lined up in a spread formation, which gave the quarterback the option to throw or run the football. Walter Johnson crouched over the football from his center position as Kelly called out the signals, took the ball from center, faked the handoff, and faded back to pass.

SAINTS
21

Running down the sidelines was Noah Franklin, the Saints' tall, lanky wide receiver, matched stride for stride by a Raiders defensive back hoping to bat away or intercept the pass. As Franklin broke into the flat, he could not break clear, and Kelly's pass was deflected away. The clock stopped when the ball hit the turf, and the referee ran it back to the line of scrimmage. It was now 2nd and 10 with 1 minute 10 seconds left.

In the huddle, Kelly said confidently, "We have all the time we need to win this game. We can't waste any more time on huddles. Everyone, remember your assignments and block hard." The team hustled back to the line. QB Rawls looked over the defense, took the snap, and pitched the ball to Danny Reeves, a fast, agile halfback. Danny ran right, faking a sweep, then pulled up and threw a perfect pass to the well-covered tight end, Ben Travis. Travis ran the ball down to the 10-yard line. It was a Saint's 1st and 10 as the clock on the scoreboard ticked away...49...48...47... The Saints were out of timeouts and lined up quickly to run another play...30...29...28 seconds.

Kelly called a play at the line of scrimmage, took the snap, and threw a pass high and to the outside. Wide receiver Noah Franklin, released from the line of scrimmage, accelerated quickly and ran a perfect fade route. He located the ball over his right shoulder, made a great catch, and stepped out of bounds on the two-yard line. The clock stopped with only 6 seconds to play. The game was coming down to one final play to determine which team would move on to the championship.

Kelly called the team back to the huddle. "We can do this," Franklin encouraged his teammates. Kelly called the play that was signaled by Coach Butler: play action right pass. The team broke from the huddle. QB Rawls called the signals and faked the dive play to the fullback, and halfback Reeves had slipped out of the backfield and was wide open in the flat. Kelly hit him with a perfect strike! The extra point was good. Final score: Saints 21, Raiders 14. The Saints bench rushed the field!

Everyone was high-fiving and jumping for joy after such a close win. Parents were slapping each other on their backs and congratulating the players. It was a total team victory. The Saints were moving on to the championship game.

After the two teams lined up to shake hands in the middle of the field, Coach Butler called the team over for a post-game pep talk.

"This was a total team win! I am so proud of every one of you. Our goal is to finish each game strong, and that is what we did today. The effort, the extra time spent in practice, and the hard work paid off. You guys can do anything you put your mind to. Never give up on your dreams. Always give God the glory in winning or losing. If your opponent falls, help him up. Always show good sportsmanship. Now, let's get ready for the championship game in two weeks. We'll take Monday off and come back stronger on Tuesday. Go Saints!"

AVIS
REEVES
18
FRANKLIN
9
21
5

Chapter 2 Making New Friends

As Kelly walked off the field with his teammates, who were still celebrating their big win, he heard several people call out his name.

"Kelly, great game! We are rooting for you in the championship!"

He turned to see a group of kids about his age standing behind a rusty chain-link fence. "The Saints can do it!" they cheered.

Kelly paused, then said to his teammates, "Guys, go ahead to the bus. I'll catch up with you later. I want to meet these Saints fans who are cheering so hard for us."

As Kelly approached the fence, he noticed the kids looked different from the friends he knew from school and the football team. Their clothes were old, tattered, and dirty. Some seemed like they might be homeless. As he looked closer, he noticed some had visible disabilities. But one thing stood out: they all wore big, genuine smiles on their faces!

"Hi," Kelly greeted them. "Did you guys see the game?"

"Yes, as best as we could," one replied. "We always watch from behind the fence."

"Why don't you come sit in the stands? You'd get a better view of the game," Kelly suggested.

"It costs $1.00 to get in," another explained. "We just don't have that kind of money. But we come most Saturdays to stand right here and cheer for the Saints."

"Wow, thank you so much," Kelly said sincerely. "I'm sorry I didn't notice you before—and about the ticket cost. Can I meet everyone?"

MATTHEW
HENRY
TOMMY
ELIJAH
MIRA
CIND
RAWLS
21
$1.00
SAINTS
8

A boy with thick glasses, held together with white medical tape and a crack in one lens, spoke first. "My name is Matthew," he said. "I don't see very well, but I love hearing the fans cheer. It makes me feel like I'm part of the team."

Next was Tommy, a big, strong-looking boy. Kelly thought, we could really use him on the offensive line for the Saints. As Tommy tried to speak, Kelly noticed he had a speech disorder, and it was hard for him to communicate. Tommy stammered, but Kelly was able to understand what Tommy was trying to say. "I, I, I, I, I, wish I could play football." His clothes appeared too small and had several patches on them, reflecting his tough circumstances.

Kelly reached out to shake hands with Henry. Henry was lame and disabled. He walked with the help of an old wooden crutch. "I'm not great at sports," Henry said, "but if you ever need help with homework, I'd love to help. My goal is to become a doctor." The group chimed in, agreeing that Henry was very smart.

Kelly then met Cindy, who sat in an old, antique-looking wheelchair with scratches and a torn wicker back. Kelly thought, she is really pretty. Her shoulder-length blonde hair and bright blue eyes lit up as she said, "Hi, Kelly! Can I get your picture?"

"Sure, you can," Kelly replied, smiling.

"Cindy is a great photographer and artist," Henry said. "You should see some of her paintings. They are beautiful!"

"Hello, my name is Mira," another girl said. Kelly noticed she had only one arm. Cindy whispered to him, "Mira's parents moved to America from Korea. They died in a car accident while she was still a baby. She has no relatives in the United States."

"I really like singing and dancing," Mira told Kelly. "Someday, I want to perform on Broadway."

Finally, Kelly met Elijah, a tall and skinny boy wearing worn-out tennis shoes held together with an electrical tape. Despite his appearance, he seemed athletic. "Have you ever played football?" Kelly asked.

"No," Elijah replied. "My caregivers said we don't have the extra money to play football. It costs too much. But I play a lot of basketball where I live. Someday, I hope to give football a try."

Kelly looked at the group. "Well, it has been nice meeting you all. Where do you all live?"

Mira replied, "We all live together in a group home about two miles from here. It is called the Carmel Road Group Home. We have several caregivers who take care of us and help with our meals."

"What about your parents?" Kelly asked gently.

"Most of us don't have any parents," Cindy said. "Or if we do, they don't want to be a part of our lives anymore."

"Can I come visit you?" Kelly asked.

"Sure," Elijah said with a big smile. "We welcome visitors any time."

As Kelly walked slowly back to the bus, he could still hear his teammates celebrating. But his mind was elsewhere, with his new friends. Despite their disabilities, poverty, and lack of family, they seemed content, even joyful. They were thankful for what little they had. Their resilience touched Kelly deeply.

A tear ran down his cheek as he stepped onto the team bus. "How can I show God's love to those in need?" he wondered.

21
SAINTS
13

Chapter 3 Who is My Neighbor? How Should I Love Them?

It was late in the afternoon, and the sky was darkening as the sun began to sink below the horizon. Kelly walked through the front door, greeted by the comforting smell of hotdogs and hamburgers. He could hear his Mom and his two grandmothers laughing and chatting about the game.

In the living room, their two cats, Winnie and Lewis, were curled up asleep on the couch. Outside, in the backyard, Kelly's Dad was playing catch with Petee, their energetic Boston terrier. Kelly loved being home. The warmth and crazy, fun moments with his family always made him feel blessed.

"Kelly, we are out on the sun porch!" Mom called out.

"Hi, everyone," Kelly said, stepping onto the porch.

"Congratulations on the big win!" Dad exclaimed, pulling Kelly into a hug. "The team played great. We are so proud of you and the leadership you showed. Coach Butler called and said it looks like you will be playing Eastover for the championship in two weeks."

"I hope everyone can come—it's going to be a big game!" Kelly said excitedly.

"We wouldn't miss it for anything," his grandmothers chimed in.

"Go Saints!"

RAWLS
21

"Dad, do you have a minute? Can we talk upstairs?" Kelly asked, his tone suddenly turned serious.

"Sure. Ladies, excuse us for a bit. We will be back down soon." Dad replied, following Kelly up the stairs. Petee chased after them.

Once they were upstairs, Dad asked, "Kelly is everything okay? I bet you are tired after such a busy day."

"Dad, I need to talk with you about something that happened after the game today. I can't seem to get it off my mind," Kelly began.

"Sure. Tell me what's going on. Let's see if I can help," Dad said with a gentle voice.

Kelly hesitated for a moment, then said, "After the game, when I was heading to the bus, I saw a group of kids about my age standing behind the fence. They had been cheering for the Saints the whole time. I stopped to talk to them and noticed something—they were different. Some of them were disabled. Their clothes were old and torn. When I asked about their parents, they said, 'Most of us don't have any parents, or they don't really want to be a part of our lives anymore.' They live at a place called the Carmel Road Group Home."

Kelly's voice wavered slightly as he continued. "They didn't even have a dollar to get into the game. But they still stood there, cheering for us. Even with everything they're going through, they seemed happy. They even invited me to visit them. At first, I was so excited after the game, but now I just feel sad. Meeting them was like looking in a mirror. It made me realize how much I've been given, and I feel like I need to do something to help them."

Dad's eyes softened as he placed a hand on Kelly's shoulder. "Kelly, you are growing up to be man with a big heart. I'm so proud of you for showing compassion for others. Let me tell you what Jesus said about loving your neighbor."

Dad read from Mark 12:30-31: "Love the Lord your God with all your heart and with all your soul and with all your mind and with all your strength. The second is this: Love your neighbor as yourself. There is no commandment greater than these."

18

Kelly nodded thoughtfully. "Dad, who is my neighbor?"

"Great question Kelly," Dad replied. "Jesus says our neighbor is anyone to whom we can show God's love. Loving one's neighbor is more than simply loving our family and friends. It means loving everyone, including our enemies. Also, our neighbor is anyone in need, regardless of their race, religion, or economic status. To love your neighbor as yourself can sometimes mean taking on the burdens of others. The Parable of the Good Samaritan is a story told by Jesus to illustrate how we should love our neighbor. Let me get my Bible, and we will read it together."

Dad flipped to Luke 10:25-37 and read aloud.

25 On one occasion, an expert in the law stood up to test Jesus. "Teacher," he asked, "what must I do to inherit eternal life?"

26 "What is written in the Law?" he replied. "How do you read it?"

27 He answered, "Love the Lord your God with all your heart and with all your soul and with all your strength and with all your mind'[a]; and, 'Love your neighbor as yourself.'[b]"

28 "You have answered correctly," Jesus replied. "Do this, and you will live."

29 But he wanted to justify himself, so he asked Jesus, "And who is my neighbor?"

30 In reply, Jesus said, "A man was going down from Jerusalem to Jericho, when he was attacked by robbers. They stripped him of his clothes, beat him, and went away, leaving him half dead.

31 A priest happened to be going down the same road, and when he saw the man, he passed by on the other side.

32 So too, a Levite, when he came to the place and saw him, passed by on the other side.

33 But a Samaritan, as he traveled, came where the man was; and when he saw him, he took pity on him.

 34 He went to him and bandaged his wounds, pouring on oil and wine. Then he put the man on his own donkey, brought him to an inn and took care of him.

35 The next day, he took out two denarii (about 2 days wages)[c] and gave them to the innkeeper. 'Look after him,' he said, 'and when I return, I will reimburse you for any extra expense you may have.'

36 "Which of these three do you think was a neighbor to the man who fell into the hands of robbers?"

37 The expert in the law replied, "The one who had mercy on him."

Jesus told him, "Go and do likewise."

22

"So, Kelly, God has commanded us to love our neighbor as ourselves. To do that, we must first understand God's love towards us. John 3:16 says, 'For God so loved the world that he gave his one and only Son, that whoever believes in him shall not perish but have eternal life. God loves us so much that he sent his only son to die on the cross as payment for our sins. The Bible tells us God's love is perfect and unconditional. It is a model for how we are to love others. 1 Corinthians 13:4-7 says 4 Love is patient, love is kind. It does not envy, it does not boast, it is not proud. 5 It does not dishonor others, it is not self-seeking, it is not easily angered, it keeps no record of wrongs. 6 Love does not delight in evil but rejoices with the truth. 7 It always protects, always trusts, always hopes, always perseveres. Imagine being loved like this…This is how God loves you! This is how God loves EVERYONE! When you have a relationship with Jesus and experience his love, you want to love others the same way."

Dad thought for a moment, then said, "Kelly let's put together a plan to share God's love with your new friends. We can be good neighbors just like the Samaritan in the parable told by Jesus. I will talk with your Mom, and I believe she will agree that this will be a great family project for Christmas. Also, I will call the Carmel Road Group Home and schedule a time to visit. We can find out what needs they may have and what we can do to help them. In the meantime, let's pray for your new friends, that they may experience God's love through us."

Dad smiled at Kelly, "I am proud of you, son. And love you!"

Chapter 4 A Visit to the Carmel Road Group Home

On Monday, the sky was covered with dark clouds. It had been raining steadily all day, and puddles were starting to form on the streets and sidewalks in Charlotte. The temperature was chilly, and there was a strong afternoon breeze blowing.

At school, the main topic of conversation was the upcoming championship game between the South Charlotte Saints and the Eastover Eagles. The Saints had the day off from practice, which gave Kelly and his family the perfect opportunity to visit the Carmel Road Group Home.

Dad had called earlier and spoke with the group home manager, Lisa Elliott. She sounded very kind on the phone and said everyone at the group home was looking forward to their visit.

As they pulled into the driveway, Kelly asked his Mom, "What is a group home?"

"A typical group home resembles a regular house located within a neighborhood," his Mom explained. "It provides support and care for people with disabilities who can't live independently. In most group homes, there are shared common spaces like a kitchen and a living room, but each resident usually has their own bedroom."

Kelly observed the house closely. It looked like a regular home with a neat, well-kept yard. But it also had features that made it more accessible—such as a ramp leading to the entrance, wider doorways, and handrails along the steps for extra support. The house was well-lit, and a small sign by the door indicated that it was a group home for individuals with special needs.

CARMEL
GROUP
HOME
25

When they arrived, Mrs. Elliott opened the front door, greeting them warmly as Kelly and his parents carried in pizza and soft drinks for everyone.

Once inside, Kelly's Mom, Donna, suggested they start by introducing themselves. "Why don't we each share one interesting fact about our lives?" she said with a smile.

After everyone got acquainted, Kelly's Dad said he had several announcements he wanted to make.

"First of all, Kelly has told me about each of you, the physical difficulties you face every day, and your interest in life. After getting approval from Mrs. Elliott, we spoke with some friends who are going to try and help you with some of your challenges in life. How would you like that?"

The students at the group home responded with an enthusiastic, "Yes!" Excitement lit up their faces, and their eyes sparkled with hope.

"In Charlotte, we are home to one of the largest pediatric hospitals in the country. Children and young adults can be evaluated and treated by some of the world's best doctors. They have doctors that can help Matthew with his eyesight and Tommy with his speech. They also have doctors that specialize in nerves, and surgeons that repair broken bones. They can help Henry and Cindy. Moreover, they have healthcare providers that make and fit artificial limbs for people like Mira. These services and treatments are being provided to you free of charge."

The group listened with amazement as Kelly's Dad went on, "But that's not all. We have some more good news! As you are aware, the South Charlotte Saints are in the championship game a week from this coming Saturday. We have found a way for everyone to be involved with the team. Tommy and Elijah, I have spoken with Coach Butler, and there are two spots open on the football team for the championship game. Two players are out with injuries, and the new rule states these players can be replaced with kids who have not played on another team this year. Coach Butler is very excited about the possibility of you guys joining the team. If you are interested, practice is tomorrow at 3:30, and we can come by and pick you up."

Kelly's Dad turned to Matthew. "Matthew, we are hoping you will assist Mr. Hilton in the press box. He does the player introductions and calls the play-by-play on the radio for the Saint's games. He has been looking for someone with a good voice. You are that person! And Henry, I have spoken with Dr. Anderson, our team doctor, and he is looking forward to you helping him on the sidelines during the game. He knows your goal is to go to medical school, and he wants to answer any questions you may have."

"Cindy," he said, smiling at her, "Donna reached out to our local newspaper and told them about your talents as a photographer and artist. They want you to take pictures and report on the championship game. They are even going to pay you for your services. Mira, the coach of the Saint's cheerleading team, is Mrs. Lewis. She is an accomplished dancer and instructor. She knows you like to dance and wants to teach you the basics of cheerleading before the big game. You can help cheer the Saints on to victory! Also, we are starting a new Sunday school class for our friends with special needs at our church. I would like to invite each of you to attend. We are going to have a lot of fun studying about Jesus, Heaven, and how to get there. Our class starts at 9:30, and Mrs. Elliott has agreed to bring everyone starting next Sunday. Can we count on everyone coming?"

The group erupted into big smiles and a unanimous, "Yes!"

On their drive home, Kelly leaned back in his seat, a thoughtful expression on his face. "I believe I now understand what the Bible says about Loving your neighbor as yourself," he said. "It means to treat the people around you, even if you don't know them well, with the same kindness and care that you want for yourself. It means to be nice to others just like you want them to be nice to you, no matter who they are!"

"Very well said, Kelly," his Dad replied. "Everyone can be your neighbor. We need to be helpful, say nice things, and listen to others. We need to be good friends! We must now follow through with everything we said to help our new friends. We need to earn their trust. We must share God's love with them. I believe we all learned today what Jesus meant when he said to Love our neighbors as ourselves."

Chapter 5 Football Practice and New Teammates

The Southpark football field was nestled in the heart of the Ballantyne community. Its well-worn grass, outlined by faded white lines, had witnessed years of youth football practices and games. Two rickety light poles stood on either side of the field, and a rusty goalpost anchored each end zone. Many generations of young men had left their mark and had become local heroes on this field.

On Tuesday, Coach Butler called a special team meeting at 3:00 to announce the additions of Tommy and Elijah to the team before practice started at 3:30.

"Many of you already know TJ and Matt are going to miss the championship game due to injuries," Coach Butler began. "TJ sprained his ankle, and Matt broke his hand in Saturday's game. Thankfully, both are going to be fine. The good news is that we have two enthusiastic young men joining our team for the championship.

"Tommy and Elijah are from the Carmel Group Home. They are special young men who come from difficult circumstances. Neither has played football before, but both are eager to learn and be part of the team. Recently, they lost their parents and have been dealing with feelings of sadness, loneliness, and uncertainty.

"Tommy has a speech disorder, and Elijah is very shy. But I believe God has given them unique talents and capabilities to fulfill their purpose in life. Remember what Jesus said in Matthew 22:37-39: 'You shall love the LORD your God with all your heart, with all your soul, and with all your mind.' This is the first and greatest commandment. And the second is: 'You shall love your neighbor as yourself.'

"Tommy and Elijah are our neighbors, and it's up to us to make sure they feel loved and appreciated as part of our team."

At 3:30, Kelly and his Dad arrived at practice with Tommy and Elijah just in time for Coach Butler to introduce them to the team. Both boys were excited to meet their new teammates and become part of the Saints.

TOMMY
ELIJAH
33

Coach Butler gave his final instructions before practice began.

"Let's work hard this week and leave everything on the field. Go Saints!"

A typical Saints football practice included warm-ups, position drills, group work, and a scrimmage. It ended with wind sprints and a cool-down. From the first day, Tommy and Elijah quickly made a strong impression on Coach Butler and his assistants.

Tommy quickly emerged as a dominant force. At 14 years old, he was already 6 ft. tall and weighed over 200 lbs. Coach Butler described him as "massive, with a strong upper body, and incredibly quick feet. He has a lot of determination and will only get better with time."

Elijah, on the other hand, was lightning-quick in practice. "Elijah may be the fastest 14-year-old I've ever seen," he remarked. "He possesses explosive speed and can run past defenders. He can change directions quickly and can cover large areas of the field. If he works hard, there is no stopping him. We have added two amazing players to our team! We will come up with several plays that will feature them for the championship game."

ELIJAH
TOMMY
SAINTS
SAINTS
35

Over the next 10 days, Tommy and Elijah made new friends and became a part of the team in every sense. They received new uniforms, shoes, and clothes for school. Their teammates invited them to dinners, movies and lunches at school. Parents and volunteers from the community prayed for Tommy, Elijah, and the other residents of the Carmel Group Home.

For the first time in their lives, they felt truly loved and wanted.

One night before bed, Kelly's Dad sat beside him and said, "Kelly, I am so proud of you and your friends. You have discovered what it means to be a good Samaritan. You have learned how to love your neighbor as yourself. I love you very much."

Chapter 6 The Championship Game

Memorial Stadium was located just minutes from downtown Charlotte, with the city's iconic skyline of tall buildings and historic structures creating a stunning backdrop. The 10,000-seat stadium has played an important role in making Charlotte a major city, hosting many important sporting events over the past decade. This was the first year the Charlotte Youth Football League championship game for 13- to 14-year-olds was being played in this historic venue.

The weather was bitterly cold, with a sharp easterly wind sweeping through the stadium. The temperature hovered in the low thirties, but the chill didn't dampen the energy of the fans. Kick-off was set for 2:00 pm between the 9-1 South Charlotte Saints and their rivals, the 10-0 Eastover Eagles. The stands were full of fans cheering, decked out in team colors, waving flags, and eagerly anticipating the action on the field.

In the Saint's locker room, Coach Butler addressed his team one final time before the big game. "To win the championship, each player on this team must stay focused, hustle, and give their maximum effort! We must play solid defense, avoid turnovers on offense, and, most importantly, have fun out there. Show good sportsmanship. Let's make this a game to remember. Go Saints!"

As the team burst out of the locker room onto the field, a familiar voice echoed over the public address system. "Welcome, ladies and gentlemen, to Memorial Stadium! Today's game between the South Charlotte Saints and the Eastover Eagles will determine the Charlotte Youth Football League championship for 13- to 14-year-olds."

Kelly, who was standing on the sidelines with his teammates, looked up and noticed that Matthew was behind the microphone in the press box with Mr. Hilton handling the public address announcements and player introductions.

"At this time, we ask everyone who is able to please rise and remove your hats for the singing of our national anthem."

Kelly turned toward the field and saw Mira, dressed in her Saints cheerleading uniform, step forward. She delivered a heartfelt performance of our nation's Star-Spangled Banner.

"Mira did a wonderful job! Her voice is so powerful and clear," Kelly's Mom remarked from the stands. She and Kelly's Dad, along with his grandmothers, were seated in the front row directly behind the team.

"I saw Henry walking on the sidelines with Dr. Anderson," Kelly's Dad added. "Dr. Anderson says he has "all the right tools" to become a doctor. Good grades, a strong work ethic, and, most importantly, a genuine passion for helping others."

At midfield, the captains of both teams gathered for the coin toss to determine which team would start with the ball. Kelly's face lit up when Cindy came out to take pictures of the coin toss in her new wheelchair. She was covering the game for the local newspaper. Watching her snap photos, Kelly thought to himself, She still looks so pretty.

The Saints won the toss and elected to receive the opening kick.

"Well, it seems like all six of our new friends from the Carmel Road Group Home are part of today's game in one way or another. What a blessing!" Kelly's Dad exclaimed. "I see Tommy and Elijah are warming up with the team, and I am excited to see them play. Coach Butler said they have done well in practice. It's been an amazing two weeks. Our community has come together and shown the true meaning of love for one's neighbor. They really are the good Samaritans!"

GREEN
38
SAINTS
21
TAY
7
42

The headlines of the sports section in Sunday's newspaper read:

Saints Defeat Eagles in Overtime to Win the Charlotte Youth League Championship

The article read:

The South Charlotte Saints defeated the Eastover Eagles 34 to 28 in overtime to win the 13- to 14-year-old Charlotte Youth League Championship.

"Nobody wanted to go home," quarterback Kelly Rawls said. "Each team played their hearts out! Our defense played great! I want to give all the credit to the Lord, my coaches, and teammates."

First Half Highlights:

In the first quarter, after forcing South Charlotte to a three-and-out to open the game, Eastover needed just three plays to march 67 yards for the opening score of the game. Halfback Justin Williams capped off the drive with a 6-yard touchdown run, giving Eastover an early 7-0 lead.

South Charlotte tied the game 7-7 when QB Rawls hit Noah Franklin with a 25-yard strike for a touchdown. It was Franklin's 5th touchdown reception of the year.

On third and 2, Eastover took the lead when starting quarterback Ronnie Bass found Terrell Brooks Jr in the end zone for a 15-yard touchdown pass with 12:28 left in the second quarter.

The Saints answered later in the second quarter when newcomer Elijah Green rushed for a 35-yard touchdown, tying the game at 14-14. Another newcomer, Tommy Taylor, made the key block that allowed Green to score.

Late in the second quarter, with less than two minutes remaining, Mark Andrews changed the momentum when he picked off a Rawls pass that had been tipped at the 26-yard line. The half ended with the game tied 14 to 14.

Second Half Highlights

Eastover received the second-half kick-off, starting at their own 32-yard line. They drove down the field on their first possession and scored a touchdown on a 14-yard run by quarterback Bass.

After a sack of quarterback Bass that would have given the ball back to the Saints, a roughing-the-kicker penalty was called against Ben Travis. The penalty gave the ball back to Eastover. The Eagles quickly drove down the field and scored a touchdown to take a 28 to 14 lead with 8:48 left in the fourth quarter.

Down two touchdowns, the Saints moved quickly and called several plays in the huddle. They went on a 78-yard drive that resulted in a 10-yard touchdown pass from Kelly Rawls to tight end Ben Travis with 2:05 remaining in the game. Eagles 28, Saints 21.

Using their three timeouts, the Saints were able to force the Eagles to punt. The Saints had a first down just shy of midfield with 38 seconds left. Elijah Green and Tommy Taylor entered the game at halfback and guard. The play sent in from Coach Butler was a triple-option right.

Quarterback Rawls called out the signals, took the snap, and faked the handoff to his fullback. He ran down the line to his right, where he was met by the Eastover defensive end. Right before being hit, he pitched the ball back to Elijah, who raced down the sidelines into the end zone for a game-tying touchdown. Eagles 21, Saints 21.

Overtime

Eastover won the toss and got the ball first, starting on the 10-yard line with four chances to score. On fourth down, Justin Williams was tackled just short of the goal line, and the Eagles failed on their chance to score.

On first down, the Saints gave the ball to halfback Danny Reeves. He gained 3 yards running off-tackle. On second and third down, the Saints failed to gain any yards as the Eagles played very tough defense. It was fourth down, and the Saints were on the 7-yard line.

As Kelly dropped back to pass, he saw Noah Franklin break free in the corner of the end zone. The pass was a little high, but Franklin reached out and made an unbelievable catch to win the game.

Final Score: Saints 28, Eagles 21

Cindy interviewed newcomers Elijah Green and Tommy Taylor after the game.

"Tommy and I are just so thankful to be a part of this amazing team. The friendships we've made will last a lifetime. Two weeks ago, we didn't feel comfortable in the community or at school. We felt alone and uncertain about our futures. Now, we feel so blessed."

Tommy stammered, "I, I, I, I, I agree with everything Elijah said. So thankful."

75
38
21
47

Chapter 7 The Parable of the Great Banquet

The next evening, Kelly's Mom and Dad brought his favorite pizza for dinner. "Congratulations on winning the championship!" his Mom exclaimed, her eyes sparkling with pride. "Did you see Cindy's article and the picture from the game in the newspaper today? It's amazing!"

"Yes, the picture she took of Tommy and Elijah on the game-tying score was cool," Kelly replied, a big grin spreading across his face.

"Coach Butler thinks Tommy and Elijah could one day get football scholarships if they work hard." Kelly's Dad added, his voice filled with pride. "They have a lot of talent."

"Mom, can I ask Cindy over for dinner one night? You can make some of your famous spaghetti." Kelly asked with a soft smile.

"Sure, you can." Mom smiled and winked as she glanced over at Kelly's Dad. "We like her a lot. It will be fun."

THE GREAT
BANQUET!
21

"Kelly, for our devotion tonight, your mom is going to read Luke 14:15-24—the Parable of the Great Banquet," his Dad began, his tone thoughtful. "In this parable, Jesus tells the story of a man who prepares a grand banquet and sends out invitations, but the guests make excuses for not attending. So, the host invites the poor, disabled, and homeless, who gladly accept. After your Mom reads this powerful passage, let's talk about its meaning and how we can apply it to our lives today."

Kelly's Mom walked over to the small table near the kitchen, where the family Bible rested, its worn leather cover a testament to years of faithful use. She picked it up carefully, flipping through the thin pages until she found Luke 14:15-24. Returning to the living room, she settled into her favorite chair, the warm light from the nearby lamp casting a soft glow on the words.

Clearing her throat gently, she began to read, her voice steady and filled with emotion:

15 When one of those at the table with him heard this, he said to Jesus, "Blessed is the one who will eat at the feast in the kingdom of God."

16 Jesus replied: "A certain man was preparing a great banquet and invited many guests. 17 At the time of the banquet, he sent his servant to tell those invited, 'Come, for everything is now ready.'

18 "But they all alike began to make excuses. The first said, 'I have just bought a field, and I must go and see it. Please excuse me.'

19 "Another said, 'I have just bought five yoke of oxen, and I'm on my way to try them out. Please excuse me.'

20 "Still another said, 'I just got married, so I can't come.'

21 "The servant came back and reported this to his master. Then the owner of the house became angry and ordered his servant, 'Go out quickly into the streets and alleys of the town and bring in the poor, the crippled, the blind and the lame.'

22 "Sir,' the servant said, 'what you ordered has been done, but there is still room.'"

23 "Then the master told his servant, 'Go out to the roads and country lanes and compel them to come in so that my house will be full. 24 I tell you, not one of those who were invited will get a taste of my banquet.'"

"Dad, what exactly does Jesus mean when he speaks of the "great banquet?" Kelly asked, leaning forward with a curious look on his face.

Kelly's Dad paused, his voice full of thoughtfulness as he explained, "The 'great banquet' represents the Kingdom of God and His invitation of salvation to everyone, regardless of race, economic status, or background. When the guests decline the invitation with excuses, it's a sign of rejecting God's grace—

prioritizing worldly things over a relationship with Him. Now, when the host tells his servant to invite the poor, the crippled, the lame, and the blind, that's God's way of showing us that He wants to include those societies often overlooked in His kingdom.

"The parable reminds us that accepting Jesus as our Lord and Savior should be a priority in life. It also teaches us to be kind to those who can't repay us, like the poor, disabled, and homeless. And, Kelly," he added with a smile, "your Mom and I have an idea. We've been thinking about how we and some volunteers from the community can celebrate Christmas this year... with the Carmel Group Home. Let me share our secret with you."

Chapter 8 A Very Special Christmas Eve

It was Christmas Eve in South Charlotte. A cold breeze was blowing, snow was sparkling under the soft moonlight, and the sky was filled with twinkling stars, creating a feeling of peace and goodwill. The outside of the old historic barn was beautifully decorated with Christmas wreaths made from fir branches with red ribbons and white candles. There was a big spruce Christmas tree with bright, colorful lights and a gold star at the top inside.

Seated around the warm fireplace, sipping hot chocolate, were the six Carmel Road Group Home residents with friends and volunteers who had gathered on this special Christmas Eve. "Kelly, our volunteers are like the good Samaritan in the parable told by Jesus. Remember, God commanded us to love our neighbor as we love ourselves. They are sharing God's love by helping those in need. Many community members have volunteered their time and money to help our less fortunate friends at the Carmel Group Home. Tonight, we are hosting a "banquet" for our special needs friends to celebrate the birth of God's son Jesus. Our volunteers prepared a traditional roast turkey, ham meal, side dishes, and desserts. "Sounds delicious, doesn't it?" Mom said excitedly. "Remember, in the parable of the "Great Banquet" the host's instruction was to invite the poor, crippled, and homeless to his party. God instructs us to be good and kind to those who cannot repay regardless of their circumstances. He wants everyone to have a personal relationship with him." Dad added.

Celebrating Christmas Eve with friends and loved ones in the barn reinforced a sense of community. The smell of Christmas food, the sound of carols, and the warm smiles on everyone's faces contributed to the wonder and joy of this special evening. After dinner, everyone sat on hay bales with quilts to stay warm. Children from a local school performed the nativity scene of Christ's birth in the breezeway. Ted stood up, lit a candle representing the Light of the World, pulled out his Bible, and began reading the Christmas story.

59

Everyone in the room sat silently, listening to his every word as he read: "And she gave birth to her firstborn and wrapped him in swaddling clothes and laid him in a manger because there was no room for them in the inn. And in the same region, shepherds were out in the field, watching their flock by night. An angel of the Lord appeared to them, and the glory of the Lord was shown around them, and they were filled with great fear. And the angel told them, "Fear not, for behold, I bring you good news of great joy for all the people. For unto is born this day in the city of David a Savior who is Christ the Lord." Luke 2:7-11.

Everyone and everything was serene and peaceful. We all sat in reverence to what we had just heard. You could almost hear angels singing in the background. As we stood singing Silent Night, the old rustic barn doors opened and hundreds of people from the community with lit candles joined in the singing. They were filled with the Christmas spirit. Their spirit reflected the love and selflessness taught by our Savior. The real meaning of Christmas became fresh and new in many people's hearts that night. It was a reminder of how much God loves each one of us.

 He answered, "'Love the Lord your God with all your heart and soul and with all your strength and with all your mind'[a]; and "**Love your neighbor as yourself.**"

SILENT NIGHT,
HOLY NIGHT
ALL IS CALM,
ROUND YON VIRGIN
MOTHER AND CHILD
HOLY INFANT SO
TENDER AND MILD
63

The Epilogue
Twenty Years Later

Individuals with special needs often possess "unlocked talents," which can manifest in areas like exceptional memory in fields like art, music and athletic ability. Recognizing and nurturing these talents early on is crucial for special needs individual growth and development. God gave them certain capabilities and talents to fulfill their calling in life. Our community learned the meaning of how to "love your neighbor as yourself." They donated their time, money and professional talents to helping those in the Carmel Group Home. Doctors, nurses, teachers, coaches, and many other volunteers showed these students how much God loves them.

There is a "Fairy Tale" ending to our story. Let's look at our six friends who were part of the Carmel Road Group Home 20 years ago and see how the Lord works in their lives. First and most importantly, all six of our friends accepted Jesus as their Savior. They became Christians and they put Jesus first in their lives. They never missed an opportunity to share God's love to others in need.

Today

1.Matthew-Matthew's eyesight improved with new glasses. He loved college football. After college, he became a play-by-play announcer for a major TV station. He is married with two beautiful children.

2.Working with several speech therapists, Tommy overcame his stuttering problem. He earned a college football scholarship and played for several years in the NFL. He is now running for a seat in the United States Congress. By the way, he is a great speaker!

3.Henry- After surgery to correct a hip that was causing misalignment and instability, Henry was able to finally put down his crutch. He graduated with a major in medical school and is now doing his residency in orthopedic surgery.

4.Cindy- With the help of several physical therapists, Cindy's mobility has improved. She can now stand on her own. She opened an art studio in Atlanta. Her art is getting national attention. By the way, she and Kelly ended up dating.

5.Mira- Mira got a new prosthetic arm that improved her quality of life. She auditioned and made the finals of a major TV talent contest. She recently signed a recording contract.

6.Elijah- Elijah took his God-given ability to run fast and earned a track scholarship to a major university out west. He went on to qualify for a spot in the Summer Olympics, where he placed third and received a bronze medal!

Each year, all six special needs friends return to Charlotte, their home, to experience Christmas in the "barn." It is a special time in everyone's life.

 In real life, Kelly went home to be with the Lord in the fall of 2022. As time passes, we often think of our fond memories with Kelly. We miss him so much! However, we rest assured that God is sovereign, and our son is now in heaven. We love you, Kelly!

You can read more about Kelly's story in "A Father's Guide to God's Promise of Heaven."

We formed Friends for Special Needs with the help of many friends and volunteers in the Charlotte community. Our mission is to improve the lives of children and adults with special needs through events and activities and provide financial support where needed. We aim to share God's love by helping those who cannot help themselves. With God's help and guidance, we have continued to grow. At our last event, we had 800 special needs caregivers and volunteers. We are blessed!

Please check out our website www.friendsforspecialneedsnc.org. Contributions can be made on the website, or you can mail a check to:

Friends for Special Needs, 1732 White Pond Lane Waxhaw, NC 28173

We will mail you a receipt. We are a tax-exempt charity. Our EIN number is 82-221143.

God's Plan of Salvation

Are you ready to make the greatest decision of your life? Are you ready to place your faith and trust in Jesus to be your Lord as Savior? All you need to do is pray a simple prayer, as Kelly did. It can be in your own words. When you surrender to Jesus, accepting his free gift of eternal life, that's the best decision you can ever make.

Parents, we look back and are so thankful. We took the time to make sure Kelly understood God's plan of salvation. We plead with you to have this conversation with your child today. This is the most important decision your child can make!

If you need help, talk with your parents, grandparents, a friend who knows Jesus, or call someone from your Church. They will be glad to help.

THE END

Love the Lord your God with all your heart and with all your soul and with all your mind and with all your strength.'[a] 31 The second is this: 'Love your neighbor as yourself.'[b] There is no commandment greater than these. Mark 12:30-31

Dedication

This book is dedicated to my beloved wife, Donna. Thanks for your unfailing love and support. You are always there for me!